GOOSED!

BY

HILLARY DePIANO

BASED ON *THE GOOSE* FROM *THE TALE OF TALES* BY GIAMBATTISTA BASILE

THE TALE OF TALES PROJECT

Giambattista Basile (1566–1632) wrote and compiled the 60 fairy tales within *The Pentamerone* (*Lo cunto de li cunti* in Neapolitan or *The Tale of Tales* in English) in Naples, Italy in the early 1600s. His sister, Adriana, published it in two volumes in 1634 and 1636 after his death. While not widely known, it's important historically because the Brothers Grimm later used it as the source for their far more famous fairy tale collection. *The Tale of Tales* contains the earliest known versions of fairy tales such as Sleeping Beauty, Cinderella, Rapunzel, Puss in Boots, Hansel and Gretel and more.

But I'm not interested in the stories everyone has heard of. I like the obscure ones, the weird ones lost to time. Why do we obsessively retell the same dozen fairy tales when there are plenty of other great ones we ignore?

It bothers me. So, since early 2013, I've been adapting these lesser-known tales for modern audiences to bring these stories back into circulation. I've modernized them with today's audiences in mind while still staying true to the spirit of the originals. Wherever possible, I also preserved the names from the original fairy tale and, where characters were unnamed, I've named them within the historical context and often with names from elsewhere in the Tales themselves.

This project is still ongoing. For the latest list of all the tales I've adapted from The Tale of Tales and what I'm working on next, visit HillaryDePiano.com.

BIBLIOGRAPHY

Basile, Giambattista (2007). Giambattista Basile's "The Tale of Tales, or Entertainment for Little Ones". Translated by Nancy L. Canepa, illustrated by Carmelo Lettere, foreword by Jack Zipes. Detroit, MI: Wayne State University Press. ISBN 978-0-8143-2866-8.

STANDALONE ONE-ACTS

There are standalone one-act versions of every fairy tale I've adapted from *The Tale of Tales*.

THE MYRTLE

30-40 minutes, 5 m 8 f (6-20+ performers possible)
A prince discovers his myrtle tree turns into a fairy maiden at sundown.

GOOSED!

(based on *The Goose*)
25-35 minutes, 2 m 6 f 8 any (11-20+ performers possible)
Two poor sisters rescue a golden goose but their sneaky neighbors want it for themselves.

ARM CANDY

(based on *Pintosmalto)*
35-45 minutes, 2 m, 4 f (5-7+ performers possible)
When a brilliant inventor builds the perfect husband out of sugar, he's stolen by a queen who wants him for herself.

THE FOURTH ORANGE

(based on *The Merchant* with characters from Carlo Gozzi's *The Love of Three Oranges)*
20-30 minutes, 4 m, 6 f, 5 any (7-20+ actors possible)
There were only supposed to be three oranges but Franceschina had to stick her nose where it didn't belong.

THE SHE BEAR

25-35 minutes, 2 m 2 f (4-10+ performers possible)
Is the prince losing his mind or has he really fallen in love with a bear?

VARDIELLO

10-15 minutes, 1 m, 1 f, 2 any
How much damage can one half-wit do before his mother gives him

the boot?

Want to combine plays to make an evening's entertainment?
You'll find shortened versions of the most popular fairy tales in this fun and fantastical full length!

THE FOURTH ORANGE

AND OTHER FAIRY TALES YOU'VE NEVER EVEN HEARD OF
100-120 minutes, 25w 12m 11any (11 to 60+ performers possible)
It's bedtime bedlam when a washed-up clown tries to sell three unruly princesses on something other than their fairy tale favorites.

Looking for something even more flexible?
Mix and match the tales above to create an evening's entertainment and I'll provide interstitial material and opening and closing scenes to connect the tales together no matter what combination you choose!

For more information about this custom option, email Hillary DePiano.

Photos by Scot Whitman, Rutgers Prep, November 2017

GOOSED!

Goosed! **premiered on November 16-18, 2017 at Rutgers Preparatory School in Somerset, NJ with the following cast and crew.**

LILLA..Paris Townsell
LOLLA ....Téa Guarino
THE GOOSE ....LongGe (Andrea) Wang
PERNA ....Elaine Rodriguez
PASCA...Selena Adrianzen
VASTA ....Esha Mehta
NEIGHBORS...Samantha Barbato, Daria
Bresnick, Carla Evans,
Kaylah Holmes,Tabetha
Kiraz, Christal
Onyekwere
PRINCE AMBROSO ....Dan Jenkins
BERNARDO ....Emmett Duffy
MIRO...Kevin Tao
MEO..Richard Xiang

ENSEMBLE
Skyllar Capuno, David Chen, Daniel Forte, Livia Lee, Nate Lyles,
Sachin Mathew, Qingshi Meng, Aarushi Roperia, Emma Sperr

Directed by ....Cora M. Turlish
Assistant Directed by ....Manuela Curutchet
Stevenson
Student Assistant Director ....Livia Lee
Set Design by ....Erin Drakoulis
Set Construction Coordination by ....Derrick Laurion
Lighting Design & Direction by ....Michael Nardulli
Costumes by ....Christina Kratzman
Stage Managed by ....Sunny Chen
Assistant Stage Manager ....Aela Williams
Lighting Board Operator...............................Jamie Chen
Sound Board Operator ....Michael Slass
Backstage Crew ....David Chen, Jonina Yang
Goose Puppet Fabrication.............................Manuela Curuchet
Stevenson
Publicity Art..Skyllar Capuno

Make Up Coordinator ....Kuntal Thakkar

Set Construction
David Chen, Jamie Chen, Jesse Cross, Liz Gambacorta, Zac Gambacorta, Libby Gilfeather, Nya Johnson, Val Lazarczyk, Matthew Romage, Rishie Seshadri, Michael Slass, Emma Sperr, Jonina Yang

Make-up
Aaditi Ahlawat, Amrin Ashraf, Mahima Chaluvadi, Rachel Emmett, Isabelle Fehl, Nithya Goel, Lauren Hanna, Catherine Harbour, Ava Margolis, Eloise Meek, Kuntal Thakkar, Tara Viswanath

~

The playwright extends her greatest heartfelt thanks to the following groups who workshopped early versions of this play. It is thanks to your excellent cast and crews that this show is what it is today!

SIERRA HIGH SCHOOL
JANUARY 11-20TH, 2017

RUTGERS PREPARATORY SCHOOL
NOVEMBER 16-18TH, 2017

ANNIE WRIGHT SCHOOLS
APRIL 26-27TH, 2018

PRODUCTION NOTES

IMPROVISATION

In the spirit of the slapstick of classic Italian theatre and commedia dell'arte tradition that inspired these adaptations, you're encouraged to put your own spin on all comedic bits and fights and to explore the physical comedy through improvisation. If you can come up with something funnier than the stage directions describe, go for it! I'm even happy to approve changes in dialog or more modern references, just run it by me first. For performer safety, avoid injury by always making sure you finalize all physical routines before the show opens. While you certainly don't have to, you're welcome to perform the show in masked commedia style if desired.

CONTENT

While this fairy tale is PG as written (as most classic fairy tales are), I'm happy to work with schools and other groups who may need to tone it down to be able to perform it. Be it language or situational, please email me (hillary@hillarydepiano.com) with any issues you run into. I'll do my best to help you find a workaround.

CASTING NOTES

I encourage blind casting in all cases where it comes to race, gender, body type, etc. If you're in a casting pickle, please email me to explain your casting needs and I'll help you out. I can give you alternate character names and lines or grant permission to change character genders as needed, whatever we need to do to make it happen.

STAGING

Staging for this play can be as simple or as complicated as you want it to be. Because of the storybook nature of the tales, costumes can be anything from elaborate period pieces to paper bag tunics with just a few elements to suggest the character. Sets can be elaborately illustrated pages from a picture book, the crayon drawings of a child's imagination or a few furniture pieces where the audience's imagination does the rest.

INCREASING OR DECREASING CAST SIZE

The neighbors' lines are numbered only as a general guideline. Please divide them up in whatever way works best for your cast. You can get away with as little as two but the chaos of the scene is funnier with a bigger crowd.

POOP

The fowl's foul excrement need not be a gross or complicated moment. While go with something simple like a silky scarf to represent the diarrhea, you can also just employ a simple sound cue and not have the goose actually excrete anything at all. The goose squats and then there's the sound of something like a slide whistle, whoopee cushion or the classic P.U. trumpet notes we all know from cartoons and then the performers' reactions and the audience's imagination take it from there.

Please don't hesitate to contact me (hillary@hillarydepiano.com) for any reason. I'm here to help!

Photos courtesy of Sierra High School Drama, January 2017

CHARACTERS
(In order of appearance)

LILLA, poor peasant
LOLLA, Lilla's younger sister
THE GOOSE, sassy fowl of unusual abilities
PERNA, Lolla and Lilla's neighbor
PASCA, Perna's older daughter
VASTA, Perna's younger daughter
NEIGHBORS
PRINCE AMBROSO, prince of the realm, totally dreamy
BERNARDO, the prince's squire
MIRO, royal guard
MEO, another royal guard

SETTING
A fairytale kingdom.

TIME
The imaginary past.

GOOSED!

SCENE 1

(A meager cottage. LILLA, waits by a small window.)

LILLA

Where is she? It's getting dark.

(Her sister, LOLLA, bursts in.)

LOLLA

Lilla!

LILLA

Gracious, Lolla, you scared me near to death. It's nearly nightfall. I was worried sick. Was there a problem with the yarn?

LOLLA

No, no. I sold the spinning right off.

LILLA

Then what in heaven's name took you so long?

LOLLA

Well, I was... Oh, it's easier if I just show you.

(She clucks her tongue.)
Here girl-girl! It's alright. Come on in. I want you to meet my big sister.

(A large goose waddles into the cottage.)

LILLA

Oh, Lolla...

LOLLA

It's a goose!

GOOSE

Honk!

LILLA

Yes. I can see that. What's it doing here?

LOLLA

She lives here now! Isn't she just the sweetest thing you've ever seen?

(She pets the goose who nuzzles her fondly.)

GOOSE

Honk.

(Lilla starts to set the table and takes out a small portion of bread. The goose falls in behind her as she moves about the cottage, mimicking her movements.)

LILLA

She's a goose like any other. Right now food would be a sweeter sight, especially when we're down to this last bit of stale bread. You best start explaining, little sister, before the growl in my belly reaches my lips. What's this?

(She catches the goose shadowing her and tries to shoes it away. The goose hops up onto the table until it's level with her face and honks at her.)

GOOSE

Honk!

LILLA

Cheeky little butt, isn't she?

GOOSE

(flattered) Honk honk.

(The goose tries to help set the table, moving cups and plates to their places with her beak and wings.)

LOLLA

Oh, Lilla, please don't be mad. I sold the yarn just like always but then there was this commotion and I turned just in time to see Prince Ambroso trot by with his train on the way to some adventure or another. And I know you'll tease me like always, but I swear he looked even more handsome than the last time and I had to watch him, just for a bit. Those eyes...Oo, they melt my innards like butter left by the fire, and under his tunic, I could just about glimpse his tight little tushie and--

GOOSE

(appreciatively) Honk honk.

LILLA

I've seen the lad myself and I am not immune to his charms but I fail to see what the firmness of the prince's posterior has to do with this beast eating the last stale crust off our plate as if it were another sister.

GOOSE

(offended) Honk? Honk!

> *(It goes back to pecking at the hard bread. Lolla*
> *catches her meaning at last and cuts it in three,*
> *giving a portion to each. The sisters and goose*
> *share the meal as they talk. The goose has*
> *surprisingly good table manners.)*

LOLLA

That's just it. I went to the butcher to get us something for the week ahead and I saw her in the pen ready for the block. She looked right at me with those sad little eyes and I realized that here I was mooning over the impossible dream of the love of a prince while all she wanted was to not end up as someone's supper.

GOOSE

(sadly) Honk.

LOLLA

I couldn't just leave her to that fate, not when it was in my power to save her. So I bought her home to live with us.

GOOSE

(happily) Honk!

LILLA

With all the money? Whatever will we live on until the next market? As if we're not struggling enough here without another mouth to feed.

LOLLA

She'll lay us some nice big eggs, you'll see.

GOOSE

(confidently) Honk.

LILLA

But until then?

LOLLA

We may just barely earn our bread, sister, but we're happy enough, aren't we? Of all the things we don't have to spare, kindness is one thing we can certainly afford. It's magic that everyone has the power to wield. Kindness is as good as gold.

LILLA

It'll probably leave its droppings all over the floor...

(The goose stops eating to glare at her.)

LOLLA

Oh, come on Lilla. Look at her. How can you send this sweet little face away?

GOOSE

(batting her eyelashes) Honk honk honk...

LOLLA

See how elegantly she pleads her case?

LILLA

Oh very well. As if I ever stood a chance with the two of you making those big eyes at me like that. Fine, the goose can stay. Heaven only knows how but we'll make it work.

LOLLA

Yay! You hear that, Goosey! You can stay! You can stay!

(She's jumping with joy and the goose joins her, flapping around and honking wildly as Lolla laughs.)

GOOSE

Honk! Honk! Honk! Honk!

LILLA

Alright, enough of that. It's late and there's a long day of spinning and chores ahead of us tomorrow.

(Lilla gets into their small pallet bed)

LOLLA

I just have to make up a bed for the goose.

LILLA

Don't bother. May as well let her sleep here with us so she doesn't get too cold.

LOLLA

Oh, Lilla! Really? I told you, Gooseykins, she acts tough, but she's really just a big softy.

GOOSE

Honk.

(The goose settles into the bed between them, nuzzling up against Lilla until she gives in and pets her head.)

LILLA

You are a sweet little thing, aren't you lass? I'll tell you this, goose, you'll be no sillier than the sister I already have.

GOOSE

Honk honk...

LOLLA

I knew you'd fall in love with her if you just gave her a chance.

(The goose sighs contentedly before falling into a rhythm of "honk-shoo" snoring)

LILLA

Silly thing. She's already asleep.

LOLLA

Look at her little face, Lilla. Have you ever seen any creature so perfectly happy?

(yawning, half asleep)
I'm so glad she's come to live with us. My belly may be empty, but I feel full, you know? Like when you're so filled up with joy that anything is possible...

LILLA

Shh, you're talking nonsense. Go to sleep. Goodnight, Lolla.

LOLLA

Goodnight, Lilla. Goodnight, Goose.

(The goose makes a soft honk in her sleep. They sleep.)

SCENE 2

(The next day. The sun rises on them all still in bed. Lolla starts.)

LILLA

Wha... what's that?

LOLLA

(waking) Hmm? What is it?

LILLA

There's something cold against my leg...

LOLLA

Oh. Gooseykins. The poor dear must have soiled the bed.

LILLA

No, it's not that it's...

*(She pulls the covers off and they gasp. Their
bed is filled with gold coins.)*

GOOSE

(trying to get their attention) Honk!

LOLLA

(doesn't notice) Gold!

LILLA

Shh! You know the big ears next door.

GOOSE

(louder) ...Honk!

LOLLA

(still doesn't notice) But there's a fortune in coins here! Where did it
come from? It couldn't have just fallen from the sky.

GOOSE

(as loud as she can) HONK!

*(The sisters finally turn to look at the goose.
With a flourish, the goose spins around and,
with an elegant squat, poops out another pile of
gold coins like those in the bed.)*

LOLLA

Oh my...

LILLA

Did it just drop that gold right from its bottom? What enchantment is
this?

GOOSE
(pushing the gold forward)

Honk...?

*(Picking up a coin with its beak and handing it
to Lilla. She examines it.)*

Honk.

LILLA

Solid gold fit for a King. I-it's a miracle! Enough to keep us in food for months. Lolla, we're saved!

GOOSE

Honk! Honk!

LOLLA

Oh, goosey, you did this for us, didn't you? To thank us. I told you kindness was its own kind of magic.

LILLA

We ought to name you Goldie, you magnificent girl!

*(The sisters embrace the goose and all three
celebrate, dancing around and laughing and
honking as the cottage scene goes dark.)*

SCENE 3

*(A few days later. The street in front of Lilla and
Lolla's house. Their next door neighbor, Perna,
sits outside with her daughters, Pasca and
Vasta.)*

VASTA

You were right, mother. Lolla's dress has been remade just as you said. I asked her myself.

PERNA

I knew it! And Lilla's is new. Second hand, but new.

PASCA

And I say you both belong in the madhouse.

PERNA

Then explain, my worthless sack of a daughter, why their bones have retreated a bit under the skin, a sure sign of regular meals? Then there's that new latch on their door as if they finally had something worth stealing. No, they've had some windfall. I'm certain of it.

PASCA

Oh, yeah? Well if they've got money now, how come they're still dressed like paupers and living in that rotting hovel?

PERNA

Because they're simple folk, Pasca. No brains, no breeding. Wealth is wasted on peasants. It would be a service for someone more experienced with comfort, such as ourselves, to liberate them from it.

VASTA

Oh goody! I was hoping that's where this was going. It's been weeks since we ran out of those coins we swiped from the miller's widow and being poor again was getting old fast.

PASCA

I'm happy enough to take whatever they've got for ourselves. Assuming there's actually anything to take in the first place.

PERNA
*(Lolla exits the cottage and begins to feed and
water their ewe.)*
Lolla. Dressed for travel, I see. Where might you be off to on this fine morning?

LOLLA

Oh. Hello, Perna. Vasta. Pasca. We're just headed to the market as soon as the chores are done.

*(Whenever Lolla isn't looking, Perna stares
pointedly at her daughters and jerks her head
towards the sisters' cottage. They are oblivious.)*

PERNA

Again? You were just there not two days before.

LOLLA

Well, uh...

(Vasta finally notices her mother's furious gesticulating)

VASTA

Mother, whatever is wrong with your head?

PERNA

(whispering) My head is fine, Vasta, it is yours and your sister's that are empty as a freshly dumped chamber pot!

PASCA

What do you--

(Perna gives them a lengthy silent lecture which consists entirely of dramatic staring and eyebrow emoting. After a few moments, they finally get it.)

VASTA

Oh!

PASCA

Got it.

(They wink back at their mother and then the two begin an exaggerated sneak towards Lilla and Lolla's cottage. Lolla meanwhile has nearly escaped back into the house when Perna addresses her again as a distraction.)

PERNA

Tell me, neighbor, how the rest of us are barely scraping by while you two are able to go shopping whenever you please.

(Lilla emerges from the cottage knocking into

Pasca and Vasta who try to play it casual)

LILLA

Come off it, Perna. It's just for a bit of thatch so the rain's not always coming in uninvited. It's not like we're off to fetch a bushel of rubies.

(During the following, Vasta climbs atop Pasca's shoulders with their version of stealth and peers above the window curtain into the house)

PERNA

So touchy. What are you hiding, I wonder?

LOLLA

Nothing! We only... That is...

LILLA

Oh, no you don't. You can just pull that nose of yours right out of our business. Lolla and I aren't doing a thing wrong. Neither of us ever came knocking on your door asking why you always seem to have more than most despite never doing a day's work. Or why whenever something goes missing around here, one of your lot always turns up with one just like.

PERNA

I don't like the meaning between your words, girl.

LILLA

Then don't start calling another's apple rotten when all can see the holes in yours. Come on, Lolla.

(As they start to walk away, Lolla whispers)

LOLLA

I don't understand! We've been so careful. We've barely spent any of the gold.

LILLA

Shhh. Big ears. We'll talk of it later.

PASCA

(whispering) Well?

> *(Vasta mimes a rather abstract goose impression)*

Are you having some kind of fit?

VASTA

(whispering) Goose.

> *(Turns back to the window and then gasps)*

What the... Aaa!

> *(Vasta screams as Pasca chucks her off her shoulders and hoists herself up on the sill for a look. Lilla and Lolla turn at the sound but cannot see Pasca and Vasta at their window from where they stand. They exchange a look and start back towards their cottage.)*

PASCA

Let me see...

> *(looks into the window)*

Holy sh--

VASTA

It!... it just...! Out of its...!

PERNA

Get over here, the both of you. They're coming back.

> *(They rush back to their mother's side. All three immediately try to look as innocent as possible as the sisters return.)*

LOLLA

Is everything alright over here?

VASTA

Gold!

PASCA

...bye! Good bye!

VASTA

Uh, yes. We just wanted you to say goodbye to your gold leavings. I mean... Good leavings... to you... because you were, you know, leaving and--

PASCA

(covering Vasta's mouth so the rest of her sentence is muffled)
Please, ignore my sister's verbal diarrhea. Um, that is... She's got the head of a goose on her and--

(With Pasca's hand still over her mouth, Vasta slaps her hand over Pasca's mouth to muffle the rest of her thought. They freeze that way for a moment before waving innocently at Lilla and Lolla with their free hands.)

LOLLA

You two are so funny.

LILLA

That's one word for it.

(quietly to Lolla)
Come. The sooner we leave, the sooner we'll be back. I'm glad we got that lock for the door. I don't trust those two any more than their mother.

(They exit. As soon as they are out of sight, Perna, Pasca and Vasta drop the pretense.)

PERNA

Well?

VASTA

It's the goose!

PERNA

Is it the sort that lays golden eggs?

VASTA

Well, no. It just sort of squats down and drops the coins right out of its bottom.

PASCA

The goose poops gold.

PERNA

Hm. That's... different.

VASTA

It's a most wondrous sight!

PASCA

And really disgusting if you stop and think about it...

PERNA

Then let's not waste any time thinking about it. Fetch my tools, girls! We haven't much time before they return and that gold must be ours!

(Exit)

SCENE 4

(A few moments later at Lilla and Lolla's cottage. The goose is napping peacefully as the three villains force the door open.)

PERNA

Where is that little feathered gold mine?

PASCA

There!

VASTA

Here goose goose goose...

(The goose awakens, jumping away from them.)

GOOSE

Honk? Honk!

(Verna and her daughters all lunge for it but they end up falling over each other trying to grab it. The goose weaves between them, escaping their grasp every time.)

VASTA

I've got it!

PERNA

No, I do!

PASCA

Get back here you stupid bird!

GOOSE
(defiant as she dodges all three)
Honk honk, honk!

PERNA

Someone grab it!

(The sisters dive for the goose but collide into each other, knocking over Perna in the process. Pasca recovers and grabs the goose's foot, but the goose slaps her with its wings until she has no choice but to let it go again. Perna grabs at its tail as it retreats. The goose turns around and chomps down on her nose.)

PERNA

Ow! Aaa! It's got my nose! Get it off! Get it off!

VASTA

I'll save you, Mama!

(She starts to tug at the goose which only makes Perna scream harder from the pain.)

PERNA

No! Stop it, you fool! You'll make a ruin of my face!

PASCA

I'll handle this.

> *(Pasca holds a broom over her head, ready to slam it down on the goose. The goose releases the nose and dodges at the last minute, so Pasca ends up hitting Vasta instead.)*

VASTA

(getting pummeled)
Ow! That's me you're hitting! Stop it!

PASCA

Where did it go?

PERNA

(nasally) Over there!

> *(The goose honks. They face off. Pasca armed with the broom, Vasta disheveled and bruised from her beating, Perna's nose gushing blood, all looking the worse for wear. The goose snaps her beak and raises her wings threateningly, think White Crane Style martial arts.)*

GOOSE

Honk! Honk honk! Honk!

VASTA

It's a monster!

PASCA

Go and get it for us, mother.

PERNA
(Clutching her ruined nose)
Certainly not. It's already developed a taste for my blood. It should be one of you.

GOOSE

(a battle cry) Hoooooooooooonk!

VASTA

I-it's charging!

(They scatter screaming as the goose runs towards them, honking menacingly all the while. It chases them all around the cottage, nipping at their bottoms whenever they let it get too close. At last, it corners Vasta and Pasca. They cower before it, and the goose gets cocky, showing off, snapping at them just to hear them scream, when Perna sneaks up from behind and traps the goose in a blanket. The goose struggles but Perna manages to keep it restrained.)

GOOSE

(muffled) Honk! Honk! Honk!

PERNA

Quickly! Spread the cloths!

(Pasca and Vasta scurry to lay the tablecloth they brought with them down on the floor.)

VASTA

Our best linens? I thought you were saving these for our dowries?

PASCA

What better way to enhance our hope chests than with a pile of gold?

(Once the sheets are set, Perna removes the goose from the sheet. She tries to escape, but they've got her surrounded. She's trapped.)

VASTA

Alright, goose. Let see those hind-quarters. Nickels and dimes too!

GOOSE

(a refusal) Honk.

(Pasca gives the goose a rough shake.)

PASCA

Come on, you stupid bird, it's time to put the mint in excrement.

*(The goose nips at her finger. She shouts and
pulls back.)*

PERNA

Oh for heaven's sake. One load, you horrible creature, and we'll be on our way. Those empty headed ninnies you live with won't even miss it.

GOOSE

(defensive) Honk!

*(The goose slaps Perna across the face with its
wing. She slaps it back and it escalates into a
ridiculous slapping war.)*

VASTA

That is not a happy goose.

PASCA

Who cares how it's feeling? The only thing that matters right now is fecal.

PERNA
*(delivering a final blow that knocks the goose
off its feet and taking out a knife)*
Enough! Open up your bowels or I'll do it for you with a knife!

*(The goose and Perna stare at each other for a
moment. The goose squats and lets out a stream
of angry diarrhea that darkens the linens. They
recoil in horror and groan with disgust.)*

PASCA

Ugh. I think I'm going to be sick. It's like liquid evil!

VASTA

I've never smelled anything so bad in my entire life. I think the hairs in my nose may have actually melted.

PERNA

We want gold and you dare to unleash this noxious stream of rot and decay?

(The goose examines the mess it made and honks proudly.)

GOOSE

Honk.

(She kicks dust over the stain and waddles off the tablecloth. As she moves, they notice the ruin of the linens.)

VASTA

(with a sob) The cloth! Our hopes!

PASCA

It's ruined! So much for our future prospects!

PERNA

First my nose and now my best linens! You'll pay for this with your life, goose!

(She rises, enraged, and dives for the goose. She grabs it by the neck. The goose is too surprised to even struggle.)

PASCA

Mother, wait!

(Perna wrings the goose's neck. It struggles for a moment and then goes still. Its tongue lolls out of its beak and its body goes limp in her hands.)

VASTA

You... you killed it!

PASCA

But what about the gold?

VASTA

What about Lilla and Lolla?

PERNA

After the trick they've played on us? I care not a fig. Let them think it wandered off.

(She tosses the goose's body out the window)
There. Into the alley with the rest of the trash.

(Vasta and Pasca stare at her)
Oh, stop your gawking. It's just a goose. Come on, we'll clean this up and search the cottage, it has to have left a few coins we can collect before the sisters return. Let them come home to neither goose nor gold and see if that doesn't serve them right.

SCENE 5

(The street outside. Perna and her daughters sneak out of Lilla and Lolla's cottage, laden with sacks of gold.)

VASTA

Hurry! I think someone's coming!

PASCA

Is that... the prince?

PERNA

Inside, quickly! We must hide our spoils!

(As soon as they disappear into their house, the Prince enters with his squire and guards.)

PRINCE AMBROSO

Just a moment, squire. Nature calls and, from the smell of this street, no one will notice if I relieve myself in that alleyway.

BERNARDO

Very well, Prince Ambroso.

*(The prince disappears between the houses.
There is some grunting that his companions try
dutifully to ignore. Silence. Then a terrible
scream.)*

PRINCE AMBROSO

Ahh! The pain! Sweet merciful gods, make it stop!

BERNARDO

Your majesty? Uh, is everything alright back there?

*(The prince emerges with the goose firmly
attached to his bottom. It flaps and kicks at him
from beneath his tunic, very much alive. It
makes an angry muffled sound as it struggles.)*

PRINCE AMBROSO

No, you fools! This damnable goose has the soft of my bottom between its beak and won't let go!

MEO

What...

MIRO

How...

BERNARDO

Why...

PRINCE AMBROSO
(wincing and writhing from the pain)

Aaa! I'd made myself a throne in that alleyway and finished my business when... Ow! ... I saw the freshly killed goose and thought its soft coat would do well for a wipe. But apparently, it wasn't as dead as it seemed. My poor bottom!

BERNARDO

That's what you get for wiping your butt with an undead goose.

PRINCE AMBROSO

What was that?

BERNARDO

I said, never fear, your highness, we'll free you!

*(They begin to tug at the goose and prince both
but the two will not separate. The prince
bellows from the pain. A crowd is starting to
gather as the neighbors come to see what all the
fuss is about.)*

PRINCE AMBROSO

Stop! You'll tear my tushie off. Aaa! I've never known such torment in
all my days!

MEO

It's no use. The beast has you like a vise!

MIRO

(drawing a sword)
I'll chop it off at the neck, my lord!

PRINCE AMBROSO

No! What if it stays clamped in death? Then they'll be no way to free
me! Bernado, plead with the crowd. See if someone, anyone, can save
me from this torment!

BERNARDO

(to the crowd)
Attention peasants! Come hither! Your prince needs your help with
what I only refer to in the most literal terms as a royal pain in the butt.

(There are murmurs from the crowd)

PRINCE AMBROSO

Tell them I'll give them whatever they want! Riches! Titles! Lands!
I'll... marriage! That's it! They'll get my hand and half my kingdom.
Anything but this wrenching pain!

BERNARDO

You hear that, folks? The way to the prince's heart is through his bottom. His highness will marry whoever can get the goose to give up its puckered prize.

NEIGHBOR 1

Let me go first! Fellow up the road told me this powder is magic.

(Throws itching powder on the prince.)

PRINCE AMBROSO

Ah! It itches! It's like I'm covered in ants.

NEIGHBOR 2

No, you old ninny. This one here's the enchanted one.

(Throws sneezing powder on the prince. He starts to sneeze.)

PRINCE AMBROSO

What was... ah... achoo! Ow! Achoo! OW!

NEIGHBOR 1

Hmm. Pretty sure that one was just flour.

NEIGHBOR 2

Oh, wait. Here's the one you're looking for!

(Throws a magic dancing powder on the prince. The prince's feet start to dance wildly as he itches and sneezes.)

PRINCE AMBROSO

My feet! I can't stop them from dancing!

NEIGHBOR 2

See? Magic.

PRINCE AMBROSO

How is this helpful? The goose is still-- And everything itches like-- Achoo! Ow! Ow-choo!

NEIGHBOR 3

(Pushing first neighbor away.)
Magic powders. Be sensible. I know just what to do, your majesty.

*(She douses the prince with a bucket of cold
water. The prince shrieks but stops itching,
sneezing and dancing.)*

PRINCE AMBROSO

Ahh! By the gods, that's cold! But at least it washed off all the powders so I'm not--

*(Neighbor 4 shoves a huge handful of herbs into
the prince's mouth. He gags on them for a
minute before spitting them out.)*
Pt-ptu! What was that even supposed to do?

(She shrugs.)

NEIGHBOR 4

I just wanted to feel included.

PRINCE AMBROSO

Wha--?

NEIGHBOR 5

Let me have a go, I've got this ointment--

NEIGHBOR 6

You already got your chance, let someone else--

*(All the neighbors start shouting over each
other, pushing and arguing over who gets to try
next. With a clamor, the crowd descends on the
prince. It's chaos as they all try their remedies,
ointments, powders, and herbs on the prince
and goose at the same time. All the while, the
prince alternately screams and sobs while the
goose flails and flaps. In the midst of this
carnage, Perna and her daughters come out of
their house, Perna with her nose over-*

bandaged.)

VASTA

What's going on?

PASCA

What are they doing to Prince Ambroso?

PERNA

Hush, girls. Let's see how to use this situation to our advantage.

(They move closer to overhear)

MEO

What should we do?

BERNARDO

He said he wanted them to try.

MIRO

But they're not going to leave enough of the prince to marry!

PERNA

Marry?

(to Pasca and Vasta)
Well? Do you want to marry the prince or not? Get in there!

*(The girls run into the throng that's
overwhelming the prince, all of them grabbing
and pulling at him as he screams and pleas.)*
Hmm. For that matter, I wouldn't mind a prince of my own either.

*(She joins the crowd. It's too much for the
prince who flails like he's drowning before the
crowd pulls him under. All that's left of him is a
single hand above the mob and even that's still
being beaten with a spring of rosemary.)*

PRINCE AMBROSO

Help! Bernado! Guards! Someone! Save me! I'm under attack!

BERNARDO

We're coming, your majesty!

MEO

Grab him!

MIRO

Save the prince!

BERNARDO

Out of the way!

> *(They dive into the fray, disappearing into the
> mob themselves. At last, the crowd parts to
> reveal the squire and servants holding the
> bedraggled prince aloft, goose still firmly
> attached)*

PRINCE AMBROSO

Get me out of here. Take me back to the palace! Perhaps the royal
doctors will have some remedy for this iron jawed fowl.

> *(As they start to march him back towards the
> castle, the crowd slows their progress, hanging
> off them and begging the prince to stay. In the
> midst of this spectacle, Lolla enters laden with
> thatch and spies the goose. She drops her
> packages and cries out.)*

LOLLA

Gooseykins!

> *(The goose lets go of the prince and turns to
> her. The crowd falls silent and follows the
> goose's gaze until everyone is staring at Lolla.
> She only has eyes for the goose.)*

GOOSE

Honk? Honk honk?

LOLLA

Silly, girl-girl. Whatever are you doing up there?

GOOSE

Honk!

(The goose flies to her and showers her with kisses.)

PASCA

Ew. No. OK, you do not want to let that thing kiss you on the mouth after where that beak's been.

(The guards lower the Prince who stares transfixed at Lolla and the goose.)

BERNARDO

If she's the goose's owner, sire, we could try her for assault on--

(The prince holds up a hand, enchanted)

PRINCE AMBROSO

With a word, her sweet voice did what potions and powders, strength and savagery could not. Look at her with that goose, Bernardo. I didn't think such kindness was even possible in this world anymore. I swear on my life that I would marry her even without the promise.

(He holds out a hand to her.)
What is your name, my dear girl?

LOLLA

Oh my goodness, you're the... L-Lolla. I mean, that's me. My name. Uh, your highness.

(She executes an awkward curtsy.)

PRINCE AMBROSO

Lolla. It rolls off the tongue like music.

(The goose steps between them, honking protectively.)

GOOSE

Honk, honk!

PRINCE AMBROSO

Is this your goose?

LOLLA

Please, sir, don't hurt her.

(She moves in front of the goose who honks defiantly from around her back.)

GOOSE

Honk! Honk honk, honk!

PRINCE AMBROSO

Hurt her? No one will ever harm a feather of that magnificent animal as long as I live.

GOOSE

Honk? Honk honk?

PRINCE AMBROSO

That goose caused me a long afternoon of utter torment and yet I would endure its grip a thousand times over now that I know it ends with my meeting you. I will treat this goose like a Queen and let it sleep on a pillow of silk for having led me to you.

LOLLA

I don't understand.

(Lilla enters, laden with more thatch, which she drops in shock as the prince drops to one knee)

PRINCE AMBROSO

I promised to marry whoever saved me from the goose and you were my savior. Lolla, will you be my wife?

LOLLA

I... Uh... I...

LILLA

By the stars!

LOLLA

Your highness, my sister...

PRINCE AMBROSO

Is welcome to come and live with us at the palace, of course. I'll find her a good match too if she likes. A gander for the goose too, while I'm at it.

GOOSE

(lewdly) Honk honk...

PRINCE AMBROSO

The three of you shall never want for anything again as long as you live.

LOLLA

I... I can't... That is, I don't...

LILLA

Lolla, don't be a fool and keep the man waiting. Let him know your heart! She's been swooning over you for years, your majesty, going on about melting innards and pert posteriors whenever you rode by.

LOLLA

Sister!

PRINCE AMBROSO

Is this true?

LOLLA

It...it is.

PRINCE AMBROSO

It is a pretty great bottom.

GOOSE

(*appreciatively*) Honk honk!

LOLLA

Oh, your highness. Nothing would please me more than to be your wife.

PRINCE AMBROSO

Then we shall be married at once! Lolla, when that goose clamped down on my cheek, I never would have dreamed it would be the happiest day of my life!

*(the two kiss passionately as the crowd "aw"s
and cheers)*

PASCA

Ugh. And now she's kissing him with that same mouth. This whole thing is so gross.

VASTA

Hush. It's romantic.

PASCA

I guess...

PERNA

Come, girls, while no one's watching, we'd best make ourselves invisible before their goose comes to cook ours.

(They start to sneak away.)

BERNARDO

What about you, little goose? Anything we can do for you for orchestrating this match?

GOOSE

Honk!

*(The goose points out Vasta, Pasca, and Perna.
They freeze. The crowd around them parts until
they stand alone. The goose slowly mimes*

*slitting their throats then lets out a single
vicious honk.)*

Honk.

BERNARDO

Wow. Uh, OK.

PRINCE AMBROSO

You heard the bird! Take them away!

MEO

Yes, your highness!

MIRO

Stone cold. Remind me never to cross a goose.

(The guards seize them.)

PERNA

Stop this! I'm not like these peasants. I come from money. I demand to
be put down at once!

PASCA

(overlapping)
It was self-defense! You don't understand, that thing is a monster!

VASTA

(overlapping, sobbing)
A duck would never do this to us!

*(They drag Perna, Vasta, and Pasca out kicking
and protesting.)*

PRINCE AMBROSO

(scooping Lolla up into his arms)
Come, Lolla, Princess of Kindness. Let me take you and your sisters,
both flesh and feathered, to the palace and your new life as my bride.

LOLLA

Oh, Prince Ambroso!

(To Lilla)
His eyes are even better up close! And the rear view's not bad either!

*(They exit, the crowd following. Lilla and the
goose are the rear of the procession.)*

LILLA

Oh, Goosey, have you ever been so happy in all your life?

GOOSE

Honk!

*(The goose squats and drops a massive gold
brick onto the ground with a clunk. Lilla picks it
up.)*
Well, there's the dowry sorted anyway. Come along, you ridiculous
creature.

GOOSE

Honk.

(Exit)

ALSO BY HILLARY DEPIANO

HILLARYDEPIANO.COM

FULL LENGTH PLAYS

THE LOVE OF THREE ORANGES

comedy / fantasy /commedia dell'arte

90 to 120 minutes, 8 f, 8 m, 5 any (13-40+ actors possible: 7-20 f, 5-20 m)

A prince is cursed to fall in love with three magical oranges.

THE GREEN BIRD

comedy / fantasy /commedia dell'arte

90 to 120 minutes, 4 m 6 f 3 any (13-40+ actors possible)

Four royals, two clowns, and way too many talking statues must unravel the mystery of the green bird before an evil queen destroys the kingdom.

ONE ACT PLAYS

DADDY ISSUES

drama

15 to 20 minutes, 1 female, 1 male, 3 any

A young woman must confront the ghost of her past.

POLAR TWILIGHT

comedy / holiday

20 to 25 minutes, 3 f, 3 m (6 actors possible: 0-5 f, 1-6 m)

Everything you know about Santa is wrong and the truth kind of... sucks. Vampire Santa Claus... but in a cute way!

NEW YEAR'S THIEVE

comedy / holiday

30 to 35 minutes, 2 m 3 f 3 any (7 to 10+ actors possible)

Someone's stolen the New Year and the main suspect is... Frosty the coat rack?

WEAK DAYS

comedy

45 to 60 minutes, 6-7 any

All five weekdays play out at simultaneously across the stage in a comic ballet. Winner of The Chameleon Theatre Circle's 16th Annual New Play Contest.

THE LOVE OF THREE ORANGES (ONE ACT VERSION)

comedy / fantasy /commedia dell'arte

35 to 40 minutes, 8 f, 6 m, 4 any (10-30+ actors possible)

A prince is cursed to fall in love with three magical oranges.

THE GREEN BIRD (ONE ACT VERSION)

comedy / fantasy /commedia dell'arte
35 to 45 minutes, 4 m 6 f 3 any (12-40+ actors possible)
Four royals, two clowns, and way too many talking statues must unravel the mystery of the green bird before an evil queen destroys the kingdom.

SHORT PLAYS (10-15 MINUTES)

THE RAVEN / LENORE
THE THREE LITTLE PIGS AND THE BIG BAD STORM
THE (COMPLETELY INACCURATE) LEGEND OF THE MUMMY WITCH HOUSE
MASKS
THE COMPLETE NOVELS OF JANE AUSTEN: NOW NEW AND IMPROVED!
THREE PADDED WALLS

OTHER FICTION AND NON-FICTION

NANO WHAT NOW?
Finding your editing process, revising your NaNoWriMo book and building a writing career through publishing and beyond.
THE AUTHOR
(award winning novella) You ever get the feeling you don't know which side of the pen you're on?

~

WRITING AS T. W. SELLER

THEWHINESELLER.COM

SELL THEIR STUFF
From eBay Trading Assistants to multichannel seller assistance, your ultimate guide to consignment selling online as a part-time income or full-time business
EBAY MARKETING MAKEOVER
Increase sales and grow traffic to your eBay items by encouraging word of mouth, focusing on your ideal buyers, and optimizing your selling for search and mobile
BEYOND AMAZON, EBAY, AND ETSY
Free and low cost alternative marketplaces, shopping cart solutions and e-commerce storefronts
THE SELLER LEDGER
An auction organizer for selling on eBay

ABOUT THE AUTHOR

Hillary DePiano is a playwright, fiction and non-fiction author best known for fantastically funny fairy tales, surprisingly sweet slapstick and unrelentingly upbeat writing advice. With over two dozen plays for everyone from pre-schoolers and up, she's honored to have had her work performed in schools and theatres around the world.

As the author of the *How to Start Writing* series, she regularly shares advice and pep as a blogger and speaker. Since 2010, Hillary heads the Northeastern New Jersey region for NaNoWriMo.org and works as a volunteer in support of their creative mission. She also writes about eBay, e-commerce, and selling online under the name T. W. Seller at TheWhineSeller.com.

For more information about her books, plays, and blogs or to connect via social media, visit HillaryDePiano.com.

www.ingramcontent.com/pod-product-compliance
Lightning Source LLC
Chambersburg PA
CBHW071843190726

48292CB00005B/1889